Wingman

Author: Jean Mills   **April 11, 2023**

In this high-interest accessible novel for teen readers, Max suspects that his friend Trace is a victim of abuse.

FORMAT	Paperback	PDF	EPUB
5 x 7.5"	9781459834323	9781459834330	9781459834347
120 pages	$10.95		

KEY SELLING POINTS

- A 15-year-old hockey player suspects his teammate is being physically abused.
- The story explores themes of bullying, friendship and how the pressure to succeed can affect teens' mental health.
- The author's previous hockey story was shortlisted for a Red Maple Award.
- The story focuses on the kindness and friendship of teammates.
- Enhanced features (dyslexia-friendly font, cream paper, larger trim size) to increase reading accessibility for dyslexic and other striving readers.

ABOUT THE AUTHOR

Photo credit: Trina Koster

JEAN MILLS is the author of a number of books for young people, including *Skating Over Thin Ice*, which was shortlisted for a Red Maple Award, and *Larkin on the Shore*. For 10 years she was part of the Media & Communications team at Curling Canada, a job that combined her love of sport with her love of writing. Jean lives in ⌐⌐⌐⌐⌐⌐

D1509544

PROMOTIONAL PLANS INCLUDE

- Print and online advertising campaigns
- Promotion at national and regional school, library and trade conferences
- Extensive ARC distribution, including NetGalley
- Blog and social media promotion
- Outreach in Orca newsletters

BISACS

YAF059080 YOUNG ADULT FICTION / Sports & Recreation / Hockey
YAF058170 YOUNG ADULT FICTION / Social Themes / Physical & Emotional Abuse
YAF058120 YOUNG ADULT FICTION / Social Themes / Friendship

RIGHTS

Worldwide

AGES

12+

orca soundings

Orca Soundings are short, high-interest novels written specifically for teens. These edgy stories with compelling characters and gripping storylines are ones they will want to read. Reading levels from grade 2.0 to 4.5; interest level ages 12+.

For more information or a review copy, please contact
Kennedy Cullen at kennedy@orcabook.com

Order online at orcabook.com or orders@orcabook.com or 1-800-210-5277

@orcabook

ORCA BOOK PUBLISHERS
orcabook.com • 1-800-210-5277

WINGMAN

JEAN MILLS

orca soundings

ORCA BOOK PUBLISHERS

Published in Canada and the United States
in 2023 by Orca Book Publishers.
orcabook.com

Library and Archives Canada Cataloguing in Publication
Title: Wingman / Jean Mills.
Names: Mills, Jean, 1955- author.
Series: Orca soundings.
Description: Series statement: Orca soundings
Identifiers: Canadiana (print) 20220250154 | Canadiana (ebook) 20220250162 |
ISBN 9781459834323 (softcover) | ISBN 9781459834330 (PDF) |
ISBN 9781459834347 (EPUB)
Classification: LCC PS8576.I5654 W56 2023 | DDC jC813/.54—dc23

Library of Congress Control Number: 2022938726

Summary: In this high-interest accessible novel for teen readers,
Max suspects that his friend Trace is a victim of abuse.

Orca Book Publishers is committed to reducing the consumption of
nonrenewable resources in the production of our books. We make
every effort to use materials that support a sustainable future.

Orca Book Publishers gratefully acknowledges the support
for its publishing programs provided by the following agencies:
the Government of Canada, the Canada Council for the Arts and
the Province of British Columbia through the BC Arts Council
and the Book Publishing Tax Credit.

Edited by Tanya Trafford
Design by Ella Collier
Cover photography by Getty Images/Boy_Anupong and Getty Images/Motortion

Printed and bound in Canada.

26 25 24 23 • 1 2 3 4

Chapter One

"We just stick to the plan, guys," says Trace. "Keep the puck in their end. One guy ready to drop back to help out Dev. Nothing fancy."

We're all at the bench, huddled close together so we can hear our captain give his pep talk. Coach Scott went over the plan first, so we know exactly what we have to do to win this game in overtime.

"And of course you guys are going to score the next goal, right?" says Dev. Yeah, we can always count on our goalie to keep things light.

He's right though. Next goal wins this second game of a best-of-three playdown. Next goal earns us a spot in the Elite Six Invitational Hockey Tournament next month in Toronto. Next goal sends the Cougars home.

"You got it, Dev," Trace says. He sticks out his glove and yells, "Hawks!"

We all lean in and mash our gloves together.

"Hawks!"

"So do you want the glory or do I get to be the hero this time?" I ask Trace as we skate to center ice for the face-off.

"I don't care who scores," he says. "You, me— Dev can score if he wants." He grins around his mouthguard. "I just want to win this game."

"Hey, Brewster. No NHL scouts here today? Just as well, loser."

Jared Colt skates by us. As usual, he skates in close and bumps Trace with his elbow. Bumps him "accidentally," just a little more than he needs to. But what do you expect from the Cougars captain and biggest jerk?

"Ignore him," I say to Trace.

"Ignore who?" says Trace, and we both start laughing.

Jared's NHL-scout comment is true though. Well, maybe not NHL scouts. But it's true that scouts from elite junior leagues have started showing up at our games to watch some of the guys in action. And that means Trace mostly. He's the best player in our league, the leading scorer, a magician with the puck.

Everybody knows he's going to be a star in the NHL one day.

He's also my captain, my centerman and my best friend. So random comments and elbow jabs from jerks like Jared Colt just make us laugh.

And pump us up to play harder.

The arena is loud and getting louder as we skate into position for the face-off. Trace bends down over his stick, not looking at anything but the puck in the ref's hand. You can tell he's ready. All he sees is the puck and that small space on the ice where it will land. I know all he's thinking about is scooping that puck back to Mitch, our defenseman. Trace doesn't hear the noise the way I do.

And it's probably just as well. Because over all the voices from our cheering section, I can hear Trace's dad yelling the loudest.

"Get the puck! Put these jerks away! You've got this!"

I look over quickly. My parents are standing right in front of Mr. Brewster, and they're cheering too, but I see them glance at each other. Everybody knows Trace's dad goes a little crazy with the team support. My guess is he already sees himself in a private box at a big arena, watching Trace score the most goals in the NHL.

So, yeah, it's loud. And on-ice rivals as well as loud fans can be distracting. It's time to shut that out and focus.

And that's exactly what Trace is doing. That's what I have to do too.

The noise from the stands gets louder as the ref blows his whistle, raises a hand and looks at both teams to make sure we're in position and ready.

Oh yeah, we're ready.

Puck drop.

Trace scoops the puck back to Mitch, just the way we planned it. Jared right away plows into Trace, of course. But Trace is too strong to be knocked over. He's also a lot faster, and he's already circling around, stick on the ice and ready for the pass.

I'm on the left wing, and I head for the Cougars blue line. I'm ready to rush into the zone as soon as the puck crosses the line. Over on right wing, Frankie hangs back, ready for Mitch's pass. All the Cougars expect the pass to go to Trace, of course, but he just fakes it. Makes it look as if he's Mitch's target.

No, it's Frankie who has the puck on his stick and races into the Cougars zone. He stops, side-steps a hit and sends the puck cross-ice to me.

Their defenseman reaches for the puck and wheels around, off-balance. Perfect!

Now the puck is on my stick, and I send it to where I know Trace will be. And he's ready.

The slap of Trace's stick. A roar from the stands as the Cougars goalie misses Trace's shot. We all hear the *ping* as the puck hits the post and bounces out.

The puck bounces straight out to Jared, who is now streaking down the ice with one of his wingers. Trace and Mitch take off after him.

Trace gets there first, of course. He's the fastest skater on the ice, but not fast enough to stop Jared from taking a shot.

Dev kicks it out. The puck comes straight back to Trace. He puts his stick down to control the rebound.

Only just as he does this, Jared shoves him from behind.

We've all caught up now. I try to slow down the Cougars right-winger with my body. We're all in our zone now. We switch to defense, but the guys are all out of position.

"Trace! Here!" I yell as I see the puck on his stick. Well, not quite on his stick. He's fighting for control.

"Back! Back!" yells Mitch. He's near the face-off circle with his stick on the ice, jostling the Cougar who's trying to take him down.

It's crazy and out of control. Not the way we planned it at all. The air is roaring. I'm not sure if that's the sound from the stands or from somewhere in my own head. I feel a surge of panic.

I see Frankie get dumped by his man, and I push and shove with the Cougars defenseman at the side of the net. Trace tries to free his stick from Jared's shove and almost gets his balance back.

The puck bounces on Trace's stick, and he tries to get it under control.

We all watch it unfold in slow motion.

The puck leaves his stick and slides five-hole, between Dev's pads, across the line and into the net.

There is silence, just for a split second.

And then it gets really, really loud.

Chapter Two

It only takes a second. It's as if time stops and we're all just frozen there on the ice, staring at the puck in the net. And then reality sinks in.

Trace just scored on our own net. We just lost the game because Trace scored a goal on our own net.

The Cougars aren't frozen though. Time starts up again, and so does the sound. Or maybe the sound was there all along and I just couldn't hear it.

I can sure hear it now.

Jared and the other Cougars are yelling those things you yell when you win. Sticks in the air. Jumping up and down in a pack.

"Hell, yeah!"

The Cougars fans are cheering from the stands. Foot stomping too. A bunch of girls are screaming.

"Whaaaaaaat?"

I guess they're happy, but it sounds more like they're terrified. I glance over at the stands. No, they're not terrified. They're happy, all right. Parents are high-fiving and clapping and yelling.

The Hawks fans are clapping too. The "support the team even when they lose" clapping. Someone calls out, "It's okay, boys. You'll get them next game." That's probably my mom.

But then I look away because I can hear one voice over everyone else's.

"What the fuck was that?"

Yes, it's Mr. Brewster. Making his feelings known.

I glance quickly at Trace. He hasn't moved. He's bent over and staring at the ice.

Yeah, he heard it too.

I skate in and tap Dev on the pads.

"It's okay, bud," I say.

Mitch is there too. And Frankie. And Shawn, our other defenseman. Dev shakes his head.

"Fuck," he says. Yeah, that just about covers it.

But then we move toward Trace, still bent over and staring at the ice. I know he can still hear his father's voice above the noise

The Cougars players start to skate back to their bench, and Jared does exactly what Jared does best. He passes by Trace just a little closer than he needs to.

"Nice one, Brewster," he says. Big grin for all of us. "Thanks, guys."

"Fuck off, Colt," I say.

"Benches!" the ref yells at us. Smart guy. He can probably see that I'd love nothing better than to slam Jared Colt and every single Cougars player in the head right now. And he knows that every player in a Hawks jersey would love to see me do it.

"It's okay, man," I say to Trace as we skate toward the bench where the guys sit slumped. Coach Scott waves us in. I can tell from his face that we're going to get the "Be positive—we get another chance" speech. Of course he's right, but it sure doesn't feel right. Not at this moment anyway.

"We'll get them next game," says Mitch. He taps Trace on the shin pad, but Trace still doesn't look up.

"It's okay," Dev says. Still no reaction from Trace. "Shit like this happens in a game. Not your fault, man."

We look at each other, confused. We're not sure what's going on with him. It's as if he can't hear or see us.

"Embarrassing!" Mr. Brewster yells, and I look up to see some of the parents turn to him. My dad says something. *Go, Dad.*

Even Coach Scott turns around. The ref skating with us toward the bench glances up. Parents sometimes cause more trouble than the players do.

Mr. Brewster raises his hands. "Okay, okay," he says. He turns and pushes his way out of the stands and up the stairs to the exit.

I glance at Trace as we get to the bench and lean on the boards so Coach can say a few words before we turn back for handshakes. Oh man. Handshakes are going to be hard after a game like this.

Trace's face is like stone. He stares at some point on the boards, not looking at anyone or anything.

"Okay, guys. You played great out there. You were robbed by a goalpost and some bad luck. Believe in yourselves. I have complete confidence in you." Coach Scott pauses and looks at Trace. "All of you."

Trace doesn't even look up.

"So handshakes, get changed, go home and relax with whatever crazy video game you guys are into now. Drink water, eat healthy food. See you at practice on Tuesday at four thirty. We'll get this done on Thursday. Right?"

"Right, Coach," we say together. Together except for Trace.

I nudge him. "Right?" I say, quiet enough that only he hears.

His eyes flick toward me, then back to whatever magic spot on the boards he's been staring at. He doesn't say anything.

"Okay, Hawks. Handshakes," says Coach. He leans in and lowers his voice. "And don't let the chirping get to you. I don't want anyone getting thrown out and missing the next game, got it?"

We all nod because we know. Here comes the chirping. Great.

The Cougars are already lined up and waiting to do the handshake line. We skate in behind Dev and start the ritual of tapping gloves and saying "good game" over and over to these jerks.

I'm in the line behind Trace. I guess he might be mumbling "good game" with every glove tap, but I'm not sure. It's torture to skate past these guys. All of them grinning. Laughing. Hooting. Enjoying how the game ended.

Yeah, there's nothing like seeing the other team's star player mess up, right?

And then we get to Jared.

"Good game," he says as he bumps Trace's glove a little harder than he needs to. He moves on to me and leans in a little so both Trace and I can hear. "Thanks, boys. That was fun!"

The ref is right there, of course. He's not stupid.

"Keep moving!" he yells as I shove Jared's glove so hard it bounces off his fishbowl helmet. We keep moving.

Fuck you, I mouth back at Jared.

Oh, it's fun, all right.

The dressing room is quiet as we get changed. Coach comes in to make sure we're moving it along, but he doesn't say anything to us. He doesn't need to.

Trace is the first one out. His hair is still plastered to his sweaty forehead as he silently stuffs his gear into the bag. He stands up and grabs his bag and sticks. He glances at me, and I think maybe he's finally going to say something.

I wait. Raise my eyebrows. Send him a silent *Hey. What's up?*

But he just looks away and walks toward the door. We hear Coach say, "Let it go, son. See you at practice on Tuesday, right?"

Maybe Trace nods or waves or something. Not a word.

Dev and Mitch and Frankie and I look at each other. The whole room pauses for a second and we're all thinking the same thing. *What's up with Trace?*

We need Trace. He's our leader, our guy. The one with the words to get us going. The one who wins games for us. The one who makes us all better.

But Trace is gone. Somewhere. One mistake on the ice, and he's gone.

What's up?

Dad texts me from the car where he and Mom are waiting for me.

Drive-thru?

Sure. I'll be right out.

I grab my stuff and stand up. Everybody seems to be moving slowly tonight, but I just want to get out of here. Burger and fries sound good to me right now.

"See you at practice," I say to the guys. Nods, a few words. "Hey, guys. We've got this, right?"

Some grins, more nods. A bit more energy as guys look up and say stuff like, "Damn right" or "Hell, yeah."

Usually it would be Trace standing here giving the pep talk. It doesn't feel right. I'm the wingman, not the captain. It's weird.

But then this whole postgame scene has been weird. Yes, I definitely need some fast food. Thank goodness I have parents who understand this.

But Trace doesn't have parents like mine. Nope.

Trace has a father who is yelling at him as I walk through the dark parking lot toward our car.

"You think that's going to get you anywhere near a pro contract? Shit like that?"

I hear them, but I can't see them. They're around the corner of the building, where it's darker. I don't know if I should go over or not. I keep walking toward our car but glance in the direction of the sound.

Yes, there they are. The dark part of the lot, near the back exit. The car trunk is open, but Mr. Brewster is in the way, so Trace still holding his sticks, with his hockey bag over his shoulder. He looks down and leans back as his dad leans in.

"Loser! Fucking loser!" his dad hisses at him, just loud enough for me to hear.

Chapter Three

"Good morning, sports fans," says Jared Colt. "Look! Here's the first star of the game."

He's walking down the hall toward Trace and me at our lockers. Two other Cougars, Chris and Parker, are with him. Yes, three smiling jerks are coming to brighten our day.

"Ignore them," I say to Trace.

I expect him to say something like he did the last time. *Ignore who?* But he just keeps his eyes on the inside of his locker.

"Nice goal last night, Brewster," Parker says. The other two laugh.

My hands curl into fists. Of course, a school hallway is not the best place to take a swing at someone. That's not my style anyway. But there's something about Jared Colt and his goons that makes me want to break the rules.

It's too bad our high school is so big that it includes students from all over the region. That means even Cougars players from the west side go to the same school as the rest of us Hawks. It makes for a lot of chirping in the hallways during hockey season.

I glance at Trace and see that his face is like stone. I can't tell if he's mad or just trying to be invisible. Usually he would turn around and say something to shut down Jared and his pet jerks.

Something like *Just being nice. You guys need all the help you can get.*

Or maybe *Yeah, the Hawks decided we wanted to play all three games. Make it worth our while.*

But he doesn't say a thing.

And there's something else. Now, as I look at him, I see a red mark, a bruise, on his cheekbone. That didn't happen during the game. It's pretty hard to get hit hard enough through a helmet and visor for it to leave a bruise.

I'm just about to ask him about it when he slams his locker shut and turns away from me. Right into Jared.

"No need to get physical, Brewster," Jared says in that voice that makes you just want to punch him. He puts his hands in the air, pretending to look scared.

Trace uses one hand to push him off. Then he steps aside and walks down the hall, away from us.

His head is down and he doesn't look at anyone, not even the group of girls who have turned at their lockers to watch the show.

"Wow," says Jared to me. "Taking it hard, isn't he?"

"Fuck off," I say, just loud enough for him to hear.

Well, maybe it was loud enough for others to hear too, because a few heads turn. There are no teachers in sight, thank goodness.

Cate Tremblay heard though.

Cate was Trace's girlfriend until about three weeks ago.

She and Trace got together at our middle-school graduation, on the dance floor. Trace had moved to town from Thunder Bay partway through that year, and he mostly just hung out with me. At grad, though, we saw a different side of him. That night all the guys wanted to dance with Cate, but Trace was the one who just walked up and asked her. And they've been together ever since.

Until three weeks ago, that is.

I didn't ask and he didn't tell. Suddenly he wasn't busy on Friday night and texted to see if he could come over and play *NHL 10*. We never played video games on Friday nights. He was usually over at Cate's. I know there's a story there, but I haven't found out what it is.

So now I look past grinning Jared and see Cate watching Trace. He doesn't look at her. Doesn't even slow down.

"Trace," she says. She reaches out a hand, but he dodges her and keeps walking.

She looks over at me.

Okay, I'm not great at reading girls. I'll be honest. But I know exactly what Cate is thinking right now.

What's wrong with Trace? What's going on?

I have no answers. Truth is, I'm asking myself exactly the same questions.

The bell goes, and even Jared has to move then. He grins in a way that makes me want to smash his mouth and then he strolls off. The hallway gets loud and busy with people slamming lockers, grabbing backpacks, running into each other as they hurry toward homeroom.

I do the same. Slam my locker and grab my pack, but when I turn, Cate is right there.

"What's going on, Max?" she asks. "With Trace, I mean. And I don't mean the game. Everybody heard about the game."

Oh, that's just great.

"Don't worry," she says. "I know you guys will win the next one. But what's with Trace? Why's he acting so weird?"

"Well, he did score the winning goal," I say as we turn to walk toward homeroom together. "For the Cougars."

She waves her hand. Waves that news away.

"I know, I know. So what? That happens, right?"

"Yeah, I guess so. But it's not great when it happens in overtime. Or when it's your star player who does it." I glance at her as we walk. She's a nice girl. You might even call her beautiful. But I've known her since we were kids in daycare, so I've never really thought of her as girlfriend material. Also she's Trace's girlfriend. Or was.

Cate shakes her head.

"Trace is a big boy. He should be able to shake that off. Come on. We know him," she says. "He's an amazing athlete. Better than anyone out there on the ice."

"Wow. Thanks."

She punches me on the arm. "Come on, Max. You know what I mean."

I do know. Trace will be playing in the NHL one day. We'll be able to say we knew him when he was a star on the hometown Hawks.

And for sure Jared Colt will go through life telling people that he knew the famous Trace Brewster too. "Yeah, he scored on his own net once during a playoff overtime. It was great! I was there!"

Jared is in my head.

"There's something…" Cate says as we reach the door of our homeroom.

There's something, all right. And it comes back in a flash of memory.

Loser! Fucking loser!

"Hey, Cate?" I turn to her. "Can we talk later? I just thought of something."

We're coming through the classroom doorway now, and I pause to let her go first. (Yes, my mom taught me to be a gentleman.) So Cate goes first, then turns to smile at me.

"Yes. Let's talk. Later."

And just as we nod at each other and turn to find our desks, I see Trace watching us.

He looks away, looks down. His mouth is set in a straight line.

I've seen that look before. On the ice. He looks like that when the ref makes a bad call. When someone on the other team takes a cheap shot at one of our guys.

Yeah, Trace is mad. At me.

Chapter Four

Trace avoids me for the rest of the day. And that's pretty hard to do because we have almost every class together. We usually sit together. We usually eat lunch together. We usually go shoot baskets during open gym time together.

We usually walk down the hall and laugh at Jared Colt and his wimpy attempts to be funny together.

Not today. Trace packs up his books and hurries out of every classroom before I can even talk to him. I'd have to sprint down the hallway to catch him.

Fine, I tell myself. Fine, Trace. Do your disappearing act. See if I care.

I eat lunch with Mitch, Shawn, Frankie and Dev.

"What's with Trace today?" asks Mitch. His mouth is full of egg sandwich. Not a pretty sight. I forgive him, though, because he's such a great defenseman.

"Probably still hurting from that overtime," says Frankie.

We nod at each other. That has to be it, right?

"Not his fault though," says Shawn.

"He's just so pissed off at himself that he needs some time to get over it," says Dev. He has already recovered from being scored on by his own player in overtime. Goalies are weird.

"Yeah, you're probably right," I say. But I don't believe it.

He's pissed off for sure. Yes, he's pissed off at himself for that big mistake on the ice. But there's something else. There has to be.

Maybe he's pissed off at me and Cate for looking all friendly as we came into the classroom this morning? Maybe it's about Jared, the chief chirper for the Cougars?

Or maybe he's pissed off at whatever or whoever gave him that bruise on his face.

But I don't say any of this to the guys.

Our last class is English. Trace is out the door and headed for his locker before I've even closed my copy of *The Marrow Thieves*. This time he's not going to escape, I tell myself.

But Cate catches me just outside the door.

"Max! Listen, we really need to talk," she says.

I hold up my hand to stop her. I glance down the hall. Yes, there he is. He's weaving in and out of the crowd, heading for his locker. I have to catch him.

"Sorry, Cate. Sorry," I say, already turning away to follow Trace. "Text me later, okay? We can talk later."

"Max! Oh, well, okay."

I hear her, but I don't even look back. Nope, I'm gone. Off down the hallway in search of Trace.

And there he is at his locker, next to mine. His backpack is on the floor. He stuffs his math textbook into it. History textbook too. He glances up quickly and sees me coming. He slams his locker door and does up the lock. Without looking at me, he slings the pack up on his shoulder and turns away.

But this time I catch up to him. I grab his arm to stop him.

"Come on, man," I say, just loud enough for him to hear me. "Come on. Wait."

I think he's going to keep going, run away again. He shrugs off my hand and starts to move away.

"Trace. Come on."

He stops and stares at the floor for moment, as if he's thinking. Maybe he's deciding whether to tell me to fuck off, I don't know. But at least he isn't running away like he's been doing all day.

"Hey, Brewster. Can I have your autograph? Star of the game, bud. Star of the game."

Great. Jared and his team of jerks just came up behind us. I didn't see them coming.

Trace looks at me then and nods his head down the hallway toward the exit. I know what this means. *Time to go. Come on.*

I nod back. Screw math and history homework for tonight. I'm not waiting around to get my books out of my locker.

Trace is already walking down the hallway, and I'm right behind him.

"Aw, come on, Brewster. You should be nicer to your fans," Jared calls after us.

We can hear him and his guys laughing, but we just ignore them. We weave our way through the hallway, down the stairs and out the exit.

Trace doesn't say anything as we head across the parking lot toward the road. There are people everywhere, of course. The usual mix of students heading home or to the bus stop.

Trace has his head down, as if he finds the sidewalk very interesting. Fine. At least we're walking together. For the first time today I'm not trying to catch up to him.

"Those guys are jerks," I say. Maybe if I get the conversation started I can get him to tell me what's going on. Maybe he'll tell me where that bruise came from.

"Yeah," he says.

Okay, it's not much, but he's talking to me finally.

Stone Road is up ahead, and I can see the parking lot of the mall. There's a little coffee shop there with the best chocolate brownies. We go there sometimes after school. These brownies are like magic. I could use some magic today.

"Hey, how about we go to the Coffee Corner?" I say. "I could murder a brownie right now."

"Sure. I guess," he says.

I'll take that as a win.

My phone buzzes, and I pull it out of my jacket pocket.

A text from Cate.

I saw you guys leave. Is he ok? Where are you going?

Mall.

See you there.

Not sure that's a great idea, but oh well. Maybe we can convince him we're not a couple, if that's what he's thinking. It would be good to shut that down. Then maybe I can find out what's really bothering him. Surely it's not all about the goal last night. And Jared and his chirping goons.

I put my phone back in my pocket. Trace hasn't even noticed. He just keeps walking, head down. So I walk along beside him and hope a chocolate brownie will work its magic.

"That *Marrow Thieves* is pretty good, eh?" I say as we wait for the light to change at the corner. I can see the mall parking lot, half-empty at this time of the day. Kids from school are heading there too. Fingers crossed Jared Colt isn't one of them.

"I guess." Trace shrugs.

We walk across Stone Road and cut through the parking lot toward the mall entrance.

"Leafs and Boston tonight," I say. Might as well keep trying. Maybe something will work.

That doesn't. He shrugs. I guess he's not planning to watch the game while doing homework.

We get to the coffee shop and line up behind a mom with a little kid in a stroller. The kid must be tired, because he's making noise and the mom keeps leaning down to say stuff to him. He looks around the edge of his stroller at Trace and me and starts to cry.

Yeah, kid. I don't blame you.

Finally it's our turn.

"Two chocolate brownies, two lattes, right?" says the woman at the counter. She knows us because we're regulars.

"That's right," I say and pull out my wallet. She smiles and goes to get our stuff.

"Wow, you're buying?" says Trace.

I almost drop my wallet. I'm so surprised that he actually said something to me. I play it cool. Maybe he's going to loosen up. Like I said, these brownies are magic.

"This one's on me," I say, nodding. "I won't forget though. You've been warned."

He doesn't say anything, but when I glance at

him, he's grinning. It's just a tiny grin. Okay, we're getting there.

I pay and we get our stuff. We walk out of the shop toward the tables just outside the door and…

We walk right into Cate.

"Oh, hi, guys," she says, but she's looking at Trace.

I don't know what happened between them three weeks ago. One minute they were holding hands and kissing at her locker when the teachers weren't looking. The next she was walking around looking sad, and he was coming over to my house on Friday nights.

But something happened for sure.

Trace freezes, brownie in one hand, latte in the other. They stand there looking at each other for a moment.

"Hey," I say. "Hi, Cate."

But before I can say anything more, he turns and walks away from us. Just like that. Not a word to me or Cate. He's gone so fast we don't have time to react.

He just leaves Cate and me standing there, staring after him.

Chapter Five

"What just happened?" Cate asks.

"I have no idea," I say.

There's no point following him. We can't even see him anymore. His disappearing act was that fast.

"Listen, Max. I was thinking," says Cate.

I nod at one of the tables, and we sit down. And yes, I break my brownie in half and push a hunk of chocolate magic toward her.

"Yum. Thanks," she says. She reaches for it but doesn't eat it right away. She's still thinking.

"What?" I say. "What were you thinking?"

"When was the last time you were at Trace's house?" she asks.

I stop chewing and think. When was it? Last week? No, he came over three times last week to play video games, and we pretended to do homework in my room. The week before? No, more gaming. And my dad drove us to practice and games that week. Trace said his dad was working late.

When *was* I last at Trace's house?

"It's been a while," I say. "That's weird. I used to go there all the time."

"I know," Cate says and nods. "It's weird that he doesn't invite you to his house." She looks down. "And it's why we broke up."

"You broke up because he doesn't invite me to his house?" I ask. This is confusing.

"No, stupid," says Cate. She hits me on the arm. "We broke up because I went to his house one Sunday afternoon a few weeks ago. I just wanted to see him." She shrugs. "Nothing big. But he told me to go away. He wouldn't let me in. He was really, really mad and he wouldn't tell me why. So we had a fight right there at his door, and then I walked away." She shrugs again and looks down.

"That sucks," I say.

She takes a bite of the brownie. Then she looks up at me. "Yeah, it sucks. And I don't understand it."

"Neither do I," I say.

"Something's not right with him," she says.

Well, duh. But I don't say that out loud.

We leave soon after. I think about asking her if she has her math and history textbooks in her backpack. Mine are still in my locker at school. It would save me a trip if she would do tonight's homework with me.

But I don't. Cate's great, but I need to think about what she said. Alone.

So I walk back to school. I check in at the front office to tell Mrs. Laski that I have to get some books from my locker.

"Really, Max," Mrs. Laski says and shakes her head at me. "You need to be more organized."

"I know," I say and smile at her. She likes me. She and my mother are in the same book club. "Do I need to sign in?"

She waves a hand at me.

"No. Go get your books and go home."

I'm reaching into my locker when I hear someone coming and look up.

Mr. Scott, the woodworking teacher at our high school. Also known as Coach Scott, the Hawks coach.

"Hey, Max," he says.

"Hi, Coach," I say.

He slows down to talk.

"Tough game last night. Is Trace okay?"

Now that is a question, isn't it?

"I think so," I lie. I could tell him that Trace was playing hide-and-seek with me all day. I could tell him what Cate and I talked about. How weird Trace has been lately. I could tell him about the bruise on Trace's face.

But as soon as you tell a teacher this stuff, everything gets messy. So I don't. Whatever is up with Trace, I'm going to figure it out.

"Well, we'll get them next game," he says. "Practice tomorrow night, right? Don't forget."

"I'll be there," I say.

Tuesday night isn't our usual practice time, but the league reserved ice time for us and the Cougars. One more practice before the final game on Thursday. The game that decides which team goes to the Elite Six tournament. We have to win.

Which means we need Trace.

I text him maybe thirty times that night.

You ok?

Sup?

Homework done?

See that goal?

Ref sucks.

Yes, I'm watching the Leafs-Bruins game and doing my math and history homework. Maybe he's doing the same thing.

One thing he's not doing is texting me back.

Another thing he's not doing is showing up for school. The next day he's nowhere around.

"Have you seen him?" Cate asks me at lunch.

"No," I say.

Maybe I should tell Coach.

That's what I'm thinking as I walk into the dressing room for practice. Because if Trace hasn't been at school all day, there's no way he'll be at practice.

But there he is. In his usual spot, next to mine. Face like stone as he puts his gear on.

Silent.

All the guys are a bit freaked out by him, I think. Nobody says much, not even Dev, our joker.

When Trace bends down to tie his skates, I look around at Frankie. Dev. Mitch. Shawn. We all just shrug at each other.

Nobody knows what to say, so we don't say anything.

Wait until we get out on the ice, I tell myself. I figure once we're on the ice again, Trace will see that we're all together. A team. He'll get back to being Trace Brewster, future NHL All-Star. He'll remember how much he loves this game.

But that's not what happens.

We're doing a penalty-kill drill, and the two of us are both following the play down the ice.

He's faster than I am, but I catch up, and we collide in the corner. He uses his stick to dig out the puck. Then he throws an elbow at my head and passes the puck to Frankie, at the circle.

"Hey, man. Elbow," I say, surprised.

He pushes off me with a grunt, and I chase him to the face-off circle. He's hoping for a cross-ice pass and the chance for a one-timer. But I tie up his stick.

He slashes my stick down, just missing my glove.

"Hey, come on. Jeez," I say. I'm confused. Elbowing and slashing aren't his usual style. He's playing like Jared or one of those players who has to hit people because they don't have the skill to play clean.

And then he turns around and cross-checks me high across my chest. So hard that I fall backward. I fall backward and it hurts.

I lie on the ice and try to catch my breath. Coach Scott blows the whistle and yells something. The guys all freeze and stare.

Trace skates to the boards. He skates fast and pushes Coach Scott's hand away. He throws open the gate and stomps off toward the dressing room.

Coach Scott follows him, leaving the rest of us staring after them.

Dev's dad is our assistant coach, and he takes over.

"Okay, boys, let's try that again," Coach Batra says. "Come on. Back to work."

We're all a bit stunned. I'm *really* stunned. Coach Batra skates over to me.

"You okay, Max?" he asks.

"Yeah, I'm good," I say. I'm back up on my skates now. I feel shaky, but not from the hit.

"Okay, face-off. Come on, boys." Coach Batra tries to distract us from looking over at the hallway and the dressing room.

I wonder what's going on in there. What the conversation is between Trace and Coach Scott.

I try to shake off the hit. Focus, I tell myself. I skate over to line up for the face-off.

But of course, I'm beside the boards.

And of course, Jared Colt and his Cougars buddies are hanging out there. They're waiting for their ice time.

"Wow," Jared says, just loud enough for me to hear. "Brewster sure has some good moves, eh, Nilson?"

And as much as I would love to climb over the boards and shut him up, I don't.

Because all I can see is my best friend's face as he took his stick and deliberately tried to hurt me.

Chapter Six

Why would he do that?

I keep asking myself this question as I lie on my bed after supper that night. I stare at the ceiling, thinking.

Maybe he's mad at me. But for what? What did I do?

I thought things were getting back to normal when we went to the mall yesterday. Then Cate showed up and he disappeared. Why?

Maybe he's mad at Cate. But for what? They broke up. Maybe he doesn't like seeing her at all.

It all started after that stupid overtime. It started after he scored on our net and we lost the game.

But wait. Maybe it started before that.

Cate asked me when I was last at his house. I can't even remember. For weeks he's been coming to my house. This is where we play video games. He's even stayed for supper a few times.

Maybe something is going on at his house that he doesn't want me to see.

I bounce off my bed and head downstairs to the back door. I grab my jacket and quickly put my boots on.

"Mom!" I yell down the stairs to the rec room, where my parents are watching the news. "I'm going over to Trace's. Back in a while."

"Okay," she calls up. "Don't be late."

"Okay," I yell back.

"Is your homework done?"

I pretend not to hear that last bit as I close the door behind me.

It's not unusual for me to go to Trace's house after supper. I used to do it all the time. But now I realize it has been weeks. Maybe even a month. The last time I was at his house, we watched some of the hockey game. His mom was working the night shift at the hospital, and we had the house to ourselves.

And then he told me he was tired. Yawned and said he was kicking me out. It was friendly and cool and everything. As I was walking home, I saw his dad drive up. Sometimes his dad worked late too, so this was nothing strange. But now I wonder if he was getting me out of the house before his dad got home.

His dad. I wonder...

It's cold tonight, and the snow has just started. I walk along the sidewalk with my hands stuffed in my pockets. It's only two blocks to Trace's house, but tonight it feels farther. I wonder what I should say to him when I get there.

Hi. Don't worry. I'm okay after that cross-check. No need to apologize for acting like a jerk.

I'm almost at his house now. The outside lights are off, but I can see lights on inside. Two cars are parked in the driveway. That means both his parents are home for once.

I stop on the driveway and plan what I'm going to do. What I'm going to say.

Ring the doorbell. When he (or his mom or his dad) answers, ask if I can come in. March into his room and tell him to grow up and stop acting like a jerk.

No. Too aggressive. That's more like something Jared would do.

Ring the doorbell. When he (or his mom or his dad) answers, ask if I can come in. Drag him to his room and get him to tell me what's going on.

Yes, much better.

I jump up the steps of the dark porch, ready to ring the doorbell.

And then I hear it.

Raised voices. Yelling. The sound of something smashing on the floor. A plate or a glass. More yelling.

"Do it right! How many times do I have to tell you, stupid bitch?"

Trace's father. Trace's father is yelling at his mom?

"Stop it!" That's definitely his mom's voice. Then a sound—she's crying.

"Don't you dare!" His dad again.

I'm frozen on the front porch. I haven't heard Trace's voice. I'm not even sure what I'm hearing. Is this an argument? Or is it a fight? Trace's dad can be a real jerk. I think back to the parking lot on Sunday night.

Yelling at people is one thing. Is it more than just yelling?

My first instinct is to run away before they know I'm there.

Instead of running away, I ring the doorbell.

Yes, that was not my first instinct. It must have been my second. Max to the rescue.

Right away it goes quiet inside. A minute ago it was loud and messy. Now it's silent.

I picture Trace's parents standing there, staring at the door. They probably hope I'm going to walk away.

But I don't. I ring the doorbell again.

There's the sound of the doorknob turning, and then Trace's dad stands there with the door only open a bit, so all I can see is him smiling out at me. I'm sure I just heard this guy yelling, and now he's giving me the friendly treatment.

"Hey, Max. Trace is busy right now. I'll tell him you stopped by, okay?"

"Um, sure. Hey—" I start. I have no idea what I should say.

But it doesn't matter because he just closed the door in my face. I'm standing on their front porch in the dark. It's completely silent inside.

Okay. I'm not sure what that was, but standing here in the dark is not going to help.

I pull out my phone and start texting Trace as I walk home.

Just at your house. Your dad said you were busy. Call me.

I don't know where he is or what he's doing. But that run-in with his dad gave me a weird feeling. I want to know my friend is okay.

Yes, he got mad and cross-checked me to the ice a few hours ago. Yes, he walked off and left me at the mall yesterday for no reason at all. Yes, he's acting like he hates me for some reason.

But he's still my best friend. I need to know that he's okay.

Much later I lie in bed, staring at the ceiling. My phone buzzes with a text.

Don't come to my house anymore.

I don't even try to text him back. Because now I know for sure that something is really wrong.

Chapter Seven

"Always fun to watch a star fall," says Jared.

The guys around him laugh. The Cougars are sitting there like a gang. They're at the next table in the cafeteria at lunch. Dev, Mitch, Shawn, Frankie and I look at each other, but we don't react.

They're talking about Trace and his meltdown at practice, of course.

"Hey, Nilson!" calls Jared. His voice is just loud enough that people turn to look. "Did Brewster get a game misconduct for that hit last night?"

"Ignore him," says Mitch.

It's hard to ignore the Jareds of the world. I want to stand up, walk over and smash my fist into his face. I'd like to feel his nose break and see blood come pouring out. All over his chin. I'd like to see his eyes go all wide and surprised.

I can't help glancing over at him. He sees me and grins.

"Hey, man, where is Brewster anyway?" he asks.

Trace didn't come to school today. This explains why the Cougars are having such a great time throwing comments our way.

"Max, just ignore him," says Dev.

"Poor guy," Jared says to his buddies. "First he doesn't know his own net. Then he starts taking goon shots at his own guys."

"Sad, really," says Parker, one of the Cougars sitting at the next table. "There goes his shot at being picked first in the draft."

"Embarrassing," Jared says, nodding. "Especially with all the hype he gets every time he steps on the ice."

"Ignore him, Max," says Frankie, beside me. He can see my fists opening and closing. "Everybody knows Trace is the best."

"This is just, you know, a blip," says Dev.

This is no blip. I haven't told the guys or anyone else about going to Trace's house last night. They didn't hear what I heard. They didn't get a text from their best friend telling them to stay away.

"We'll tell you all about the Elite Six tournament, okay, guys?" says Jared, and his gang laughs.

I stand up so fast that my chair almost falls over.

Fuck off, I mouth at Jared and give him the finger. Then I grab my pack, stuff the rest of my lunch into it and walk out of the cafeteria without saying another word to anyone.

I run straight into Cate.

Maybe she's been watching the little show Jared was putting on and saw me getting more and more pissed off. It's as if she was waiting for me.

"Ouch!" she says, stepping back and rubbing her arm. But she also smiles a little.

"Shit! Sorry," I say. "I didn't see you."

"I could tell," she says, nodding toward Jared. "Assholes can have that effect on people."

"Yeah, well," I say. I turn and start walking away from her, but she reaches out and grabs my arm.

"What happened?" she asks. "With Trace, I mean. Something's happened, hasn't it?"

"I went to his house last night," I say. "I wanted to ask him what the hell is going on with him."

She nods. "Yeah, that scene at the mall was pretty weird," she says. "So you went to his house. And?"

"And I hear noise inside. Loud voices. Swearing. And then his dad opens the door and says Trace is busy."

Cate nods again, slowly.

"So I text him and call him all night." I shrug.

"Nothing, right?"

"Right. Nothing." I pause, thinking. Should I tell her?

"What?" Cate looks at me. "Nothing? Really?"

Why are girls so smart?

"Nothing except a text telling me not to go to his house anymore. And then he's not at school today." I shrug and shake my head at her. "I just don't understand. He went nuts at practice and nearly took my head off with an elbow. And then he cross-checked me. And then he just left the ice."

Cate nods. "I know. The anger. The 'stay away' text. I know all about it."

We look at each other.

"I don't know what to do. Should I tell someone? Who would I even tell?"

Getting the adults involved is not my first choice. Especially when I'm starting to think that adults might be the problem in the first place.

"You know, the same thing happened to me," Cate says. "He stops answering my texts or calling me. Then he stops coming to my house. Then he tells me to stop coming to his house."

I nod. "Okay. Weird."

"As if, I don't know, as if he's afraid to have me there," she says.

I think about the loud voices I heard at Trace's front door last night. I picture his dad in the parking lot after that shitty game on Sunday.

"And skipping school," Cate says. "Come on. He's not that guy. It's just not like him. Something's up."

No kidding.

We stand there, trying to figure out what to do next, and then Cate says, "You know, there was this time we were talking. I told him about my treehouse, when I was little. Remember my treehouse? It's where I always went when my parents yelled at me or I had a fight with my sister. I called it my safe place."

I nod because I remember her treehouse. It was awesome. I'd begged my dad to build me one too, but we didn't have a tree big enough.

"Okay," I say. What does this have to do with anything?

"And he said, 'Oh, for me that would be the arena.'"

We look at each other for just a second. Then I turn away and start to run down the hall.

"Do you want me to come too?" she calls after me.

Too late. I'm gone.

Chapter Eight

I make a quick stop at my locker to grab my jacket and think about throwing a couple of books into my pack. I can check with the guys later to see if there's any homework from our afternoon classes.

Screw homework. I leave the books behind, slam my locker shut and head for the exit.

The exit opens up into the parking lot. So yeah, I don't pass the front office, and I don't sign out either. Mrs. Laski will be very disappointed in me. Again.

I also don't run into Jared and his gang, and that's a good thing. I'm worried about Trace, yes. But I'm so pissed off at the Cougars and the fun they're having putting Trace down. Putting our whole team down, really. It would take just one wrong word from Jared to make me ram my fist into his face. And man, that would feel so good.

But it would get me into so much trouble. So no Jared is a good thing.

Hey, I'm all about competition. And having a cross-town rival has always been good for our team. It gets us up for games. Gets us ready for the next battle on the ice. But the latest war seems to be all about Trace. And now Trace is in trouble.

So the Cougars can go screw themselves. I'm going to find Trace and figure out why he has cut himself off from his team and from Cate.

Why he's cut himself off from me.

It's snowing when I step outside. Gray, windy and snowing. And of course the arena is on the other side of town. Yup, I have to walk for about an hour into the cold November wind.

"Trace, buddy," I say under my breath. "When we finally figure this out, you owe me."

I turn onto the sidewalk and start walking fast, head down.

An hour of walking goes by quickly when your head is full of words and images.

Like Trace's text. *Don't come to my house anymore.*

Or Jared, standing at the boards after that cross-check. *Wow, Brewster has some good moves, eh, Nilson?*

Trace's dad. *You think that's going to get you anywhere near a pro contract? Shit like that?*

Words are bad enough, but my head is full of pictures too.

The puck sliding between Dev's pads and into the net.

Trace standing in the dark parking lot as his dad yells him.

Jared's sick smile as he comes toward us in the hallway at school the next morning.

And Trace's face as he cross-checks me to the ice. More angry than I've ever seen him before. Angry at me? Maybe angry at himself.

I'm frozen and covered in snow by the time I get to the arena. I expect it to be empty and quiet, but no. There's music playing over the loudspeaker. I walk by the little counter where they sell hot chocolate and snacks during hockey games. Mrs. Ferris is on duty. She's doing something to the coffee maker and doesn't see me go by. This is good, because she might ask questions. *Hi, Max. Why aren't you in school?*

I push open the heavy doors that lead to the

ice surface and get hit with the music. Oldies, the radio stations call it. The ice is full of skaters, and it looks like I have just crashed a party for grandparents. Gray hair, warm sweaters and coats, a few hockey jerseys, lots of helmets, hats and mitts. They skate along in groups and in pairs. Some are alone, but they seem to be enjoying themselves. I'm impressed with their style as I stop at the glass. I watch them for a minute, thinking.

I need to figure out where to look for Trace.

An old lady wearing a Winnipeg Jets hockey sweater slides by on figure skates and smiles and waves at me through the glass. Okay. I wave back.

Somebody's grandpa sees this, and he waves at me too as he whizzes by.

Then two old guys in ski jackets catch sight of me and take a break from talking to smile at me. Nice style, both of them. Maybe hockey players in the Old-Timers League.

Okay, enough of this. I can't stand here watching old people skate to hits from the '60s and '70s all day. I need to find Trace.

I back away from the glass and look around. Where to start?

The dressing rooms. Maybe he found an empty dressing room and is hanging out there, out of sight.

I hurry around the boards and toward the hallway with the dressing rooms.

The door is propped open at the first dressing room I come to. When I look in, I see a few of the old-timers sitting and talking. Some are putting on skates, or maybe they're taking them off. It's hard to say.

"Hi, there," a man with white hair and big glasses says.

"Oh, hi," I say and back out of there quickly. I don't want to have to answer any questions about why I'm here at the arena in the middle of a Wednesday afternoon and not in school. For all

I know, these people are all retired teachers and principals.

"Looking for something?" the man asks, but I don't reply.

The next room has no people, but boots and a few coats are lying around.

The next dressing-room door is locked. I try it twice. Same for the next room.

Is Trace hiding in there? Should I knock?

"Hey, how's it going, Max?" says a voice, and I jump.

It's Wally, the Zamboni driver. He has popped his head out of his office just down the hall from the dressing rooms.

"Uh, hi, Wally," I say. I try to sound all cool and calm, but so many things are going around in my head. Like, is Wally going to ask why I'm not at school? Or does Wally know I am here because his spy, Mrs. Ferris, told him I was running around the dressing rooms during Old-Timers Free Skate?

Does he think I'm planning to steal stuff from the dressing rooms?

But really I'm not worried. I know Wally is a good guy. Sometimes he lets the Zamboni warm up for a few minutes and gives us extra time on the ice. He stands at the glass and cheers us on at games. (True, he cheers for everyone. Even the Cougars, but still.) He always waves at the little kids who press their faces up to the glass between periods as he goes around and around on his big machine. Wally is a bit of a celebrity at the arena.

Now he smiles at me and waits.

"You need help with something, Max?" he asks after a few seconds of silence. I have no idea what to say.

"Uh, no. I was just…I was just…" I know I sound like a loser.

But Wally doesn't seem to notice. He just nods toward the end of the hall. "Try the storage room," he says.

"Oh," I say. "Okay." Does he know what I'm looking for? *Who* I'm looking for?

He nods down the hall again.

"It's okay, Max. I think Trace could use a friend right now."

Chapter Nine

I open the door of the storage room.

Trace is sitting on one chair with his feet up on another. His laptop is open on his lap, and he has a big cup from the concession stand on a pile of boxes beside him. He looks up and freezes as I stand in the doorway.

"Surprise," I say.

He stares at me, eyes wide, and I realize something.

Trace is scared.

"So can I come in?" I ask.

He lets out a big breath and shrugs. He looks away from me.

"Sure. If you want," he says and squints at his computer screen as if something important is happening there. I hear the theme music for one of our video games.

Okay. We're going to play it like that, are we? Fine. Time to get serious.

"What the fuck is going on?" I ask.

That gets his attention. He stares at the computer screen for a moment longer and then he takes a deep breath and lets it out. He looks at me.

"Wally?"

I grin at him. "Yup. Wally."

I lift a chair off the pile in the corner and sit with my feet up on another pile of boxes that all say *Benson's Hot Cocoa Mix* on the side.

"Good old Wally," says Trace. He closes his laptop and reaches for the cup beside him. Takes a sip. "He brought me this."

"Maybe I should go get one from Mrs. Ferris," I say. "Party time in the storage room."

"Wait long enough and maybe Wally will bring you one too," says Trace. We grin at each other.

This feels almost normal, but I know it's not.

"So really," I say. "What's going on?"

"You don't want to know," says Trace, and he looks away.

"You see? That's the thing," I say. "I *do* want to know. I want to know why you're skipping school. And running away from Cate and me at the mall. And jeez, man, that cross-check. What was that?"

He doesn't look at me. I'm not sure he's looking

at anything, really, as he sits there. His eyes are on his closed laptop, but I don't think he sees it.

Silence.

And then we both jump as the door opens.

A hand holding a cup appears. And then Wally looks around the edge of the door. As he pushes it open, we see that he holds two cups.

"Thought you might need a refill," he says as he comes in and hands one of the cups to Trace. "And here you go, Max. Keep him company." He hands me the other one. "It's going to get busy around here in another hour or so. Mrs. Ferris will be getting supplies for the concession. And the CanSkate instructors keep their stuff in here too." He nods at some orange pylons stacked in the corner. "So maybe think about heading out soon. Okay, boys?"

"Yeah, sure. Thanks, Wally," says Trace.

"Thanks, Wally," I say.

He nods at us both as he heads back out the door.

"Good guy," I say after the door closes. I take a sip. "The best hot chocolate comes from arena concession stands, I swear."

"Agree," says Trace.

We grin at each other.

And then I stop grinning and say, "So what the fuck was that cross-check about?"

A long silence. I'm prepared to wait as long as I have to. It's time to find out what's going on, and I'm going to sit here until I do.

Finally he looks up at me.

"Sorry," he says in a low voice. "Sorry about that."

I nod. Okay, we're getting somewhere.

"It's just…it's just…everything is so fucked up right now," says Trace in a voice I've never heard from him. Hard. Angry.

"So tell me then. Tell me what's going on," I say. "Maybe I can help. Or somebody can."

He sighs and closes his eyes.

"You can't help. I don't think anyone can, but, okay, all right. You want to know, and I'll tell you. I'm scared my dad's going to do something bad," he says.

His dad? Yeah, his dad has been known to do crappy things like yell a lot at hockey games. And yell a lot after games. And yell in the house when people like me are standing at the front door.

"Bad. Bad like how bad?" I ask.

"Bad. Like hitting-people bad," says Trace.

I glance at the fading bruise near his eye and then at him. He's watching me, I guess to see if I understand what he's saying.

"Your dad hit you, didn't he," I say.

He nods.

"Not the first time," he says. "But he hit me and then when Mom tried to stop him, he hit her too."

Shit.

"When?" I ask.

"Sunday night, after that fun game where I scored the winning goal," he says.

"You have to tell someone," I say. "I can tell my parents. Tell Coach. Somebody needs to know."

"And then what?" asks Trace. "He says, 'Oh, sorry. I won't do it again,' and then he does it again. We've been down this road before."

"You have?" I ask.

"Yeah, before we moved here." Trace sighs. "When we lived in Thunder Bay. He got laid off from work and started drinking, and it got bad. He didn't touch me, but Mom got it from him."

He closes his eyes and shakes his head, as if he's trying to shake away the memory.

"Mom told him the drinking had to stop or she would leave and take me with her," he says. "And he got better. And when we first moved here, he was good. But now…"

Trace shrugs.

"Now it's bad again," I say, and he nods.

"It's bad. And it's my fault."

"Your fault?" I squint at him. "Why?"

"Because the scouts come and tell him I'll be in the NHL. Because he thinks when I'm a star in the NHL, I'll be rich and famous so he'll be rich and important too," Trace says through clenched teeth. He's angry now. "The scouts say all this stuff to the parents, you know? Coaches and scouts have been calling our house since I was seven, maybe younger. They search out kids, did you know that?"

He looks up at me, shaking his head. "Some are good, but some of these guys are just looking for talent they can turn into money. And my dad likes money and everything that comes with it. Cars. Big house. Lots of booze too. Partying. I don't know where he gets this idea from. The idea that I'm going to be the next McDavid, or Matthews, or Crosby, or Gretzky." He stops and wipes his hands over his face. Like he's wiping away dirt.

"Maybe because you are actually good enough to be the next NHL star?" I shrug. "But still…"

"I just want to play for fun," he says quietly. "I love this game. I just want to play. And win. And yes, making it to the NHL would be a dream, but not if I have to take my dad along with me. And I told him that."

Trace shakes his head again.

"So after that game last week, and that stupid goal, we got into it. He yelled at me in the parking lot after, and I could tell he'd been drinking," he says. "And then we got home and started in on the NHL stuff and I told him to fuck off and just let me play, and he hit me."

"Shit," I say. This is getting worse and worse.

"And then Mom stepped in and he slapped her and they started yelling," he says. "And after that, I kind of shut down. Went to my room. Locked the door. I hardly remember going to school on Monday, if you want to know the truth."

He looks up at me. "I kept thinking if I dropped out of hockey, that would be like a kick in the teeth to my dad. And I'd enjoy it. I was so mad." He looks down again and mutters, "So mad."

"I could tell," I said. "Cate and I, we were worried about you."

Cate.

"Speaking of Cate, you guys broke up, and I know it's none of my business, but did something happen?" I ask.

Trace looks at the floor and shakes his head again.

"She came over one night to watch the game with me, and my dad came into the room. He was drunk. After she'd left, he said…" Trace looks at me. "He said she was hot. 'She's hot. Nice piece of ass, eh, son?' I thought, No way I'm going to let him anywhere near her. So I told her we were over."

That is so screwed up I hardly know what to say. We sit there in silence for a moment.

"You were protecting her," I say.

"I was trying to." He shrugs. "Not sure anybody won there."

We sit in silence again.

"And the cross-check," Trace finally says. "I don't know. I just snapped. It all built up inside me, and I just exploded." He looks up at me and shrugs. "And you were there, in the way, so you got it all."

I nod at him. "I get it. No harm done." And then I grin at him. "Watch your back though. Payback coming, buddy."

And for the first time in over a week, he laughs. Okay, not an all-out, ha-ha-ha laugh, but enough to tell me he's finding his way back.

We hear raised voices in the hallway outside, and we both turn as the door bursts open.

Trace's dad is standing there, Wally right behind him.

Chapter Ten

"There you are," says Mr. Brewster, smiling at us from the doorway. "I thought I might find you here."

Trace and I freeze as his dad takes a few steps into the room. He has his car keys in his hand. He must have just come in from the parking lot.

He looks normal. He doesn't look like a guy who drinks too much, hits his family and says creepy things about his son's girlfriend.

"Thanks, Wally." Mr. Brewster turns and nods at Wally, who is standing behind him in the doorway. "Wally didn't want to tell on you, but I persuaded him."

Wally's face is white. He's mad—or scared. I can't tell which. He looks at Trace and me and shrugs a little. I'm pretty sure he means he's sorry.

"The school called to say you were absent," Mr. Brewster carries on in this friendly voice. Too friendly. He grins at Trace. "I was pretty sure I'd know where to find you, right, son?"

Then he turns to me, still smiling. Okay, it's a smile. But it's also weird and scary. Think the Joker from Batman.

"Didn't know you'd be here too, Max, but I guess skipping school is more fun with a friend, right?" He laughs.

No one laughs back. Do I smell booze?

"So come on, Trace. Let's go." He nods toward the hallway. "Big game tomorrow. You too, Max.

Better get home and eat a big supper and get a good sleep, right?"

Trace doesn't say anything but drops his feet off the chair and starts gathering his things. He slips his laptop back into his pack. He doesn't look at me.

I wish he would look at me though. I'd say something like, *Don't go with him. Come home with me. We'll figure this out. We'll talk to my parents. You can't go home with him.*

Mr. Brewster may be smiling and friendly right now. He may be giving good advice about getting ready for the game tomorrow. But I don't trust him.

Trace stands up and pulls on his jacket. He slips his pack onto his back. He still doesn't doesn't look at me as he goes out the door and into the hallway. He doesn't speak, but his dad does.

"See you tomorrow at the game, Max," he says, smiling, and turns to follow his son. "Thanks again for your help, Wally."

I smell the booze on his breath for sure now. I grab my jacket and pack and glance at Wally as I turn to follow them.

Wally isn't smiling. His face is tight, and his mouth is set in a straight line. He touches my arm on the way out.

"I'm sorry, Max," he says.

"Not your fault, Wally," I say.

Wally nods down the hall. Trace and his dad have disappeared around the corner.

"I guess Mrs. Ferris said something about Trace being here when his dad walked in. Told him to ask me." He frowns. "I could lose my job if I don't tell parents where their kids are."

"Hey, Wally, not your fault," I say again. "Listen, I gotta go. Thanks, eh?"

I'm desperate to follow Trace and his dad outside. I have a bad feeling about all this.

"Be careful, Max," says Wally as I hurry away from him.

It's noisy in the arena. Happy old-timers and their music are still going strong. I hardly look at them as I speed past on my way to the exit.

Outside it's dull and gray. Late afternoon. The snow swirls around, and the streetlights have already come on. I had no idea we had been in Trace's hiding spot for most of the afternoon. With the low clouds and blowing snow, it seems later than it is.

I see them right away.

They're in the arena parking lot, standing beside the Brewsters' red SUV. Mr. Brewster has his door open, as if he's ready to get in. But he's turned toward Trace, who stands a little away from the car, not moving. I can't hear their voices. They're too far away.

They don't see me standing at the corner of the arena. I walk a little closer. I'm still next to the wall of the arena, behind some bushes. I'm hidden. It's a perfect place to spy on them.

"Come on, quit messing around," I hear Mr. Brewster say. His voice is different now. It's not that smiling, fake-friendly voice he used back in the storage room.

Trace doesn't move. He says something, but I can't hear what it is.

Mr. Brewster steps away from the car.

"You're asking for it," he says, louder. "Get in the car. Now."

Trace takes a step back.

Mr. Brewster takes a look around the parking lot. The old-timers aren't out yet, and the little kids in CanSkate haven't arrived. It's quiet, with no one around but me. I'm sure he can't see me against the wall of the building, behind the bushes. He suddenly reaches out and grabs Trace's arm.

And what do I do? I run toward them. I don't even think about it.

Trace tries to pull away, but his dad whips him around and hits him, hard, across the head.

Trace staggers and nearly falls. But his dad holds him up and hits him again. He starts yelling too.

"You don't ever speak to me like that, hear? You lazy little shit. More talent than any kid on the ice and you don't even care. No NHL scout is ever going to look at you!"

"I don't care!" Trace yells back.

I don't even think about what I do next.

"Stop it!" I yell as I shove Mr. Brewster so hard that he staggers back and lets go of Trace. "Leave him alone!"

Mr. Brewster didn't see me coming, so he's off-balance for a moment. Just long enough for Trace to get back on his feet and start running.

Trace runs across the parking lot toward the park with its trees and paths and no roads for cars.

"Go, Trace!" I call out just as Mr. Brewster takes a swipe at my head too. He misses mostly. I turn on him.

"Fuck off!" I yell.

I think he might try to hit me again, and I'm ready. The blood pounds in my ears, and I plant my feet, ready to take him on.

But he stops. Maybe he realizes that hitting kids in a wide-open public space is a bad idea. He staggers a little and steps back toward the open car door. He drops his car keys and has to bend over to pick them up.

He's drunk, I think to myself. This asshole is not only trying to beat up his own son and his son's friend, but he's driving around drunk.

Keys in hand, Mr. Brewster stands up and leans toward me.

He gets into the car and glares back at me.

"Watch yourself, Max. This is personal family stuff. None of your business." He slams the car door shut, starts the engine and screeches out of the parking lot.

"Loser!" I yell after him.

And then, without another thought, I run back into the arena to find Wally.

Chapter Eleven

"He hit him!" I yell as I burst through the door of Wally's office.

"Who?" Wally asks. He's sitting at his little desk. He turns quickly and frowns at me. "Trace?"

"Trace's dad!" I'm still yelling. I can't catch my breath. It's weird, because I didn't run that far.

Wally stands up quickly and puts his hands on

my shoulders. He makes me sit down on the other chair in his office.

"No! Wally! We have to find Trace!" I stand right back up. I have to make him understand.

"Trace hit someone?"

"No! His dad! Mr. Brewster hit Trace. And then he tried to hit me."

Wally reaches for the phone.

"Where's Trace now?" asks Wally.

"He ran away, into the park," I say. Why am I having so much trouble catching my breath?

My legs suddenly feel weak, and I sit down. Wally nods at me. "Sit, Max. Take slow breaths. It's going to be okay."

Is it? Is it going to be okay? I just watched my best friend get hit by his own father and run off into the park. His dad could be chasing him right now.

And Trace's dad is also drunk. Mr. Brewster

could be driving through red lights and running people over on sidewalks.

"Wally, we have to do something," I say. My voice doesn't sound like my voice at all. Is this what it feels like to have a panic attack, I wonder?

But Wally is already on the phone, and he nods at me. He holds up a hand.

"Yes. This is Wally Kemper at the Pine Hill Arena," he says into the phone. "I'd like to report an assault."

I know I should stay and answer questions and say what I saw. I know the police will probably come and need to talk to me. I'm a witness, right?

But I don't care. As soon as Wally says that bit about reporting an assault, I'm out of there.

I run down the hallway and around the rink. I don't even glance at all those old-timers having fun on the ice. You don't know how lucky you are, I think.

I hear Wally yelling at me to come back. But I don't. I run. I have to find Trace.

I slam out of the front doors of the arena and into the snow, and I run toward the park. Maybe he's hiding there.

Of course, I take a quick look around the parking lot as I run, just to make sure Trace's dad isn't still parked there. Waiting for Trace. Maybe waiting for me.

No red SUV. I run through the parking lot in the same direction Trace took and follow the first path that runs through Pine Hill Park.

I stop by the first group of trees and grab my phone to text Trace.

You ok? I'm in the park. Where are you?

I wait a moment to see if he replies. Of course he doesn't. I start running again.

It's getting later and darker now. The lights along the path have come on. I run past a couple of people walking dogs, but that's all. As I run past the empty playground and the picnic area and the baseball diamond, I look around to see if I can spot

Trace anywhere. Maybe he's hiding in the trees. Maybe he's just sitting somewhere, waiting for all this to go away.

I come out on the other side of the park and onto the street.

Shit. No sign of him. I check my phone. Nothing.

Should I go home? No. By now I bet Wally has called my parents, and they'll be looking for me too. Who knows? Maybe Mrs. Laski has called them, too, to report that I skipped school.

Like magic, my phone buzzes. Mom.

Where are you? Are you OK? Need to talk.

Wally or the school must have called her. Forget it. I need to find Trace. But if I don't reply, she'll go nuts.

I'm fine. On my way home, I lie. That should give me some time.

And then she calls. I hit the red Decline button. I stuff my phone in my pocket.

Where could Trace be? I ask myself over and over. Where would he go?

Cate. Would he go to Cate?

I stop and grab my phone again and try to catch my breath.

Have you seen Trace?

It only takes a minute for her to reply.

No. Why?

Should I tell her? Yes, I should tell her. She knows him as well as I do. My phone buzzes again.

Did you find him at the arena?

Yes. His dad came. Hit him. Trace ran away. Can't find him. Any ideas?

She doesn't text me back. She calls.

"Have you tried his house?" she says.

"No," I say. "Why would he go home?"

"If his dad is all fired up and hitting people, Trace will be worried about his mom."

Smart. Cate knows Trace, that's for sure. Why didn't I think of that?

"Okay," I say as I start to run again. "Thanks."

"I'm—" she starts, but I've already clicked off.

My phone buzzes in my hand, and I glance at it quickly. Is it Trace finally?

No, it's Cate again.

Meet you there.

Fifteen minutes later I stand across the street from Trace's house and try to catch my breath. The front door is closed, and the curtains are pulled shut in the front room too. I wonder what's going on in there right now.

The red SUV is in the driveway.

And so is a police car.

I hear footsteps running toward me on the sidewalk and turn to look. There's Cate, with her jacket open and a woolly hat with a Leafs logo pulled over her long hair. She looks like she got ready in a hurry.

"You were fast," I say.

"Thought you might need backup," she says. "What's happening?"

"I don't know," I say. "I just got here."

"Cops," she says. "Did you call the cops?"

I shake my head.

"No, that was Wally at the arena," I tell her. Good old Wally, who will probably be mad at me for running off like that. Too bad. I'll say sorry next time I see him.

I'll say thank you too.

"Look," says Cate, nodding across the street.

The front door of the Brewsters' house has opened, and Mr. Brewster is coming out. But he's not alone. Two cops come out with him, and one holds him by the arm. The other one stands on the porch and turns. She says something to someone inside. I see Mrs. Brewster and Trace come to the door and stand there talking to her. Trace has his arm around his mom's shoulders.

"Oh," breathes Cate. "I hope they're okay."

Me too. But I don't say anything. I wonder if Trace has noticed us standing here watching.

The cop says something we can't hear, and she nods at them and follows her partner and Mr. Brewster to the car. She opens the door to the back seat, and her partner guides Mr. Brewster inside. She slams the door and waves once more at Trace and his mom, standing in the doorway. Then the two officers get in their car and drive away.

It's very quiet on the street. The snow is still falling, but the wind has dropped now.

"I feel like I'm standing in a snow globe," says Cate.

"Do you think they can see us?" I ask.

"I don't know," she says. "Should we go over?"

"No, I don't think so," I say. "Let's give them a minute."

Cate and I watch as Mrs. Brewster turns and hugs Trace. Then she goes back inside.

Trace stands at the door, looking out through the snow. Can he see us standing here? Of course he can. It's not as if we're hiding. Is he mad that we're standing here, watching the show?

He doesn't move. He stands there looking out. Looking out, maybe, at Cate and me. And then he raises his hand and waves at us.

Once. Twice.

I raise my hand and wave back.

Then he steps back inside and closes the door.

Chapter Twelve

It's quiet in the dressing room.

Sure, there's the sound of guys pulling on equipment and sweaters, lacing up skates. But no one is talking much. There's not much to say. We all know we have to win this game.

And Trace is there too, sitting in his usual spot beside me.

I didn't hear anything from him last night or this morning. I texted him a few times. Nothing. I had no idea if he would show up this afternoon or not.

But he did. He walked in, dropped his hockey bag on the floor and started to change.

Now he sits beside me and unties his skates and ties them up again. It's one of his good-luck routines. Usually someone will chirp him about this weird habit, but not today.

Trace hasn't said a word since coming into the dressing room.

Dev catches my eye. He raises his eyebrows and points his chin at Trace. *Is he okay?*

I shrug back. *He's here, isn't he?*

He may not be saying much, but Trace is sitting here with us, getting ready to play. That has to be a good sign, right? After all that's happened in the past couple of days?

Through the door we can hear the Cougars come out of their dressing room across the hall and start yelling as they walk toward the ice. Their skates make dull thumps on the padded carpets.

"Cougars! Come on! We got this!" All that rah-rah stuff. Getting themselves pumped up. They thump their sticks on the floor and make a lot of noise.

As soon as it gets quieter, Dev looks around the room at everyone and says in a bored tone of voice, "Cougars suck." And we all start laughing.

I glance at Trace. He's still looking down at his skate laces and not laughing.

"Hawks rule!" yells Frankie, and everybody joins in with that crazy-loud chanting we always do.

Well, everybody except Trace. But when I look at him, I see him give a small nod and glance my way.

And then he stands up and looks around the room. Everybody goes quiet and looks at him, and I know we're all waiting for him to do what he always does. The big speech, the pep talk. Telling us we got this. Leading us out onto the ice. Showing everyone why he's our captain and the best player out there.

He doesn't do that though. He looks around the room, gives a big nod and heads toward the door.

Dev, Mitch, Frankie, Shawn and I are the first ones on our feet to follow him out the door, down the hallway and onto the ice.

And, of course, as soon as Trace's skates touch the ice and he starts his first swooping circle of the warm-up, Jared and his jerks are ready.

"Oh, look," says Jared, just loud enough for us to hear. He and his two wingers have timed it so that they pass close by Trace and me at center ice. "We're counting on a couple of goals tonight, Brewster. Thanks in advance."

Trace ignores them, but I smile at Jared as

if he just said the nicest thing ever. I slow down, and he slows down. And then I say, "Fuck off," and, still smiling, I skate away.

"Not much else you can say to guys like that," Mitch says as he skates up beside me. We tap gloves and laugh.

I laugh, sure, but to be honest, I'm nervous about what's coming.

The last time I was on the ice with Trace, he tried to take my head off with a cross-check. That practice was a disaster. Our last game was a disaster.

And so much has happened since then. I have no idea what's going to happen next.

The ref blows his whistle to signal the game is about to start, and both teams go to our benches for last instructions.

"You know what to do, guys," says Coach Scott, looking around at all of us. "You know what we have to do to win this game. We play as a team.

Shoot the puck in and chase it. Puck possession wins. Protect Dev. And take shots—take lots of shots and grab those rebounds. You're the better team here, and I have complete confidence in you."

He looks at Trace then, but Trace is staring at a spot on the bench.

"Come on. Let's hear it," he says. "Hawks!"

"Hawks!"

We yell it louder than I've ever heard it before.

Trace is still in some zone of his own as he skates to center ice and gets into position for the face-off against Jared. The ref says the usual thing about playing clean. I'm over on my wing, and I can see Jared roll his eyes at that.

He catches me watching him and grins.

And then...

The ref drops the puck. Trace wins the face-off and snaps the puck over to me. He skates past Jared, heading for the blue line. He taps his stick on the ice once, and I make the pass, right to his stick. He dekes around the Cougars defenseman. Then he toe-drags the puck and goes to his right. With a sudden shift to the left, he puts the puck on his backhand.

And then, as the Cougars goalie realizes he's gone the wrong way and reaches with his stick to make the poke check, Trace roofs it.

Six seconds. It took Trace six seconds to score a goal.

The arena is suddenly loud with all the Hawks fans screaming and clapping. The guys on the bench bang their sticks and gloves on the boards and yell at the tops of their voices. My parents are standing and cheering, and I see Mrs. Brewster standing with them.

And right beside her is Cate, jumping up and down and yelling, "Traaaaaace!"

Of course, all of us rush up to Trace and just about tackle him.

"How did you do that, man?" yells Frankie, hugging him.

"Yes! Yes!" That's Dev, yelling from his goal crease at the other end of the ice.

We do our glove taps down the bench with the rest of the team, and I expect Coach to make a line change, but he doesn't.

"Get back out there," he says to us and nods toward center ice. I can see Jared standing there. His face is red, and he's chewing his mouthguard in anger. I'm sure he's saying very bad words in his head right now. I love it.

So the five of us skate back toward center ice to line up for the face-off. But just as he passes me, Trace bumps me with his elbow.

I look at him. He nods.

"Thanks, man." He says it quietly so no one else can hear. "Thanks for not giving up on me."

Before I can say anything, he skates back into

position, stick on the ice, eyes on the puck in the ref's hand.

But then, quickly, he looks over at me and grins. I grin back.

My best friend is back. And we're exactly where we should be. Him at center, me on his wing.

Trace turns his eyes back to Jared, who is glaring at him. He gives Jared a huge smile. Oh, yeah. Jared is steaming mad. If the ref wasn't standing between them, I'm pretty sure the swear words would be flying out of Jared's mouth.

But Trace? There are so many things Trace could say right now. But he just smiles and doesn't say a word. He doesn't need to.

Acknowledgments

I've been around hockey all my life but never as a coach, so a big thank-you to my nephew Eric Mills, whose many years of experience as a "hockey dad coach" helped me with details about minor hockey on-ice action, equipment and dressing-room expectations. I may have tweaked those details to serve my story, so any mistakes are completely my own.

Jean Mills is the author of a number of books for young people, including *Skating Over Thin Ice,* which was shortlisted for a Red Maple Award, and *Larkin on the Shore.* Her latest novel, *The Legend,* is set in the world of sports media, a world Jean knows well from her years spent working in communications for Curling Canada. Jean lives in Guelph, Ontario.

The Adventures of Alianore Audley

Brian Wainwright

BeWrite Books, UK
www.bewrite.net

Published internationally by BeWrite Books, UK.
32 Bryn Road South, Wigan, Lancashire, WN4 8QR.

A CIP catalogue record for this book is available from the British Library

First published in Australia by
Jacobyte Books, 2002

ISBN 1-904492-78-9

Also available in eBook format from www.bewrite.net